THE BOY OF THE THREE-YEAR NAP

Dianne Snyder   Illustrated by Allen Say   Houghton Mifflin Company   Boston

Library of Congress Cataloging-in-Publication Data

Snyder, Dianne.

The boy of the three-year nap/Dianne Snyder; illustrated by
Allen Say.

    p. cm.

    Summary: A poor Japanese woman maneuvers events to
change the lazy habits of her son.

    HC ISBN 0-395-44090-4   PA ISBN 0-395-66957-X

[1. Laziness — Fiction. 2. Japan — Fiction.] I. Say, Allen, ill.
II. Title.

PZ7.S68518Bo   1988   87-30674
[E] — dc19   CIP
               AC

Printed in the United States of America

BVG 10 9

To Jeanine, Amy, and Ross

—D.S.

To my daughter, Yuriko

—A.S.

On the banks of the river Nagara, where the long-necked cormorants fish at night, there once lived a poor widow and her son.

All day long the widow sewed silk kimonos for the rich ladies in town. As she worked, her head bobbed up and down, up and down, like the heads of the birds hunting for fish.

"What next? What next?" she seemed to say, as if the work would never end.

Her only son, Taro, was, oh, such a clever lad and as healthy as a mother

could wish. But, alas! He was as lazy as a rich man's cat. All he did was eat and sleep, sleep and eat.

If he was asked to do any work, he would yawn and say, "After my nap."

It was said that if no one woke him, Taro would sleep three years at a stretch. And so he was called "The Boy of the Three-Year Nap."

When Taro was nearly grown, a rice merchant moved to town and built a mansion. It had twenty rooms with sliding doors that opened onto the most exquisite garden. In the center was a pond filled with golden carp. And at the end of the garden was a teahouse where one could sit in the cool of the evening and gaze at the moon.

The merchant's wife and daughter wore elegant kimonos with obis of gold brocade. The merchant himself carried a cane made of ivory and smoked a pipe with a bowl of solid gold.

Taro was impressed with his fine new neighbors and began to sneak into the garden between his naps. Everything he saw enchanted him — the magnificent house, the elegant daughter, the fat carp in the pond.

When the merchant counted out his sacks of rice with a tap of his cane, Taro would sigh. "Ah, what a life!"

As the months passed, Taro grew even more lazy. His mother began to pester him, first in one ear, then the other.

"I hear the merchant is looking for a boy to work for him," she told Taro.

"What does he need a boy for?" Taro asked.

"To haul rice sacks, what else?" said the mother.

"Hauling rice sacks!" Taro laughed. "I pity the fool who takes the job. His back will get bent like an old man's."

"How can you sit here and do nothing?" she cried. "The roof leaks like a basket, the walls are crumbling, the rice sack is empty. I don't know how we shall live. I don't know how!"

"Cheer up, Mother. I have a plan."

"How you talk! What you need is a job, not a plan!"

"Don't worry, but you must make me a black kimono and hat like a priest wears."

"What will you do with them?"

"Oh, they are part of my plan." That was all he would say.

"Maybe he is planning to become a priest," Taro's mother thought. But the priests she knew got up before dawn, ate only one meal a day, and never took naps. Try as she might, she could not imagine her son doing that. Still, she decided to make the kimono and hat, for she did not know what else to do.

The next evening, Taro put on the new clothes. Then, with a piece of charcoal, he blackened his brows and drew scowl lines on his forehead and on each side of his nose. When he was done he looked as fierce as a samurai warrior.

"Taro, is it really you?" his mother cried out.

"Don't be alarmed, Mother," said Taro. "It's all part of my plan. Now, don't say a word of this to anyone."

Before she could say more, he ran out of the house.

13

At sundown, the merchant came out of his house for his evening walk.

"Good evening, madam," he called to Taro's mother. "I suppose that lazy son of yours is still in bed."

"He's a little tired tonight, sir," said the widow.

"Ha! You are a soft one. What he needs is a good smack on his back and a kick on his bottom. Napping at dusk, indeed!"

The merchant went on his stroll until he came to a shrine by the roadside. It was the shrine of the ujigami, the patron god of the town. As he stopped to make an offering, a black figure appeared before him, scowling like a goblin.

"Wh——who are you?" asked the startled merchant.

"I am the ujigami," a fierce voice bellowed.

"What do you want of me? What did I do?" cowered the merchant.

"It is time for your daughter to take a husband," said the ujigami. "You must wed her at once to that fine lad who lives on your street."

"What fine lad, my lord?"

"That fine young man called Taro."

"Taro!" The merchant rubbed his ears. "You mean 'The Boy of the Three-Year Nap,' *that* Taro?"

"The same!"

"Oh, no! There must be some mistake!"

"Gods do not make mistakes!"

The merchant began to tremble. "Surely there must be someone else my daughter can marry. Anyone but Taro —"

"Not a one," growled the ujigami. "It has been decreed, ordained, and sanctified!"

"Oh, my lord, grant me time to think about this. Couldn't we wait a year or two?"

"Impudent mortal!" the ujigami thundered. "How dare you bargain with me! If you delay my command, I shall turn your daughter into a cold clay pot! See if she can find a husband then!"

"No, no!" wailed the merchant. "My child, a pot? Have mercy!"

Falling on his knees, the merchant beat his fists against the ground and sobbed until he was quite worn out.

By then, however, the god had disappeared.

19

Quite early the next morning, the merchant came knocking on the widow's door. His eyes were red and his face was drawn, as though he had cried all night.

"Madam, I come on the most urgent business," he said grimly. "It seems that my daughter must marry your . . . ah . . . son."

The poor woman's mouth fell open.

"Yes, your son," the merchant repeated. "The ujigami appeared to me last night, and that is his command."

"But the ujigami has never appeared to anyone before," the widow exclaimed.

"That was so, until last night. I am ruined."

"Tell me, honorable sir, what did the god look like?"

The merchant shivered. "In dress, he is like a priest. But in manner, he is more like a goblin. His face is as black as coal and as fierce as a warrior's."

The widow saw at once what her son was up to. Her head began to bob up and down, up and down — like a cormorant about to dive after a fish. Still, she did not want to seem too eager.

So she said to the merchant, "We are humble folk, my good sir. My Taro could never marry a lady as fine as your daughter."

"Agreed," the merchant cried. "But unfortunately what we think matters not. We must do as the god commands or he will turn my daughter into a clay pot."

"How terrible!" The widow widened her eyes. "But, sir, even if they are to marry, your daughter could never live in this wretched house. Why, the roof leaks in a hundred places, and the walls have so many cracks the wind blows right through."

The merchant frowned. He had not thought of that.

"Very well then, I will send a man to mend the cracks and leaks," he said.

23

First thing the next morning, a plasterer came to repair the house.

"Fine work, fine work," Taro mumbled from his bed.

In the evening the merchant said to the widow, "Now will you consent to the marriage?"

"Alas, how can I, sir?" The widow bowed. "As you can see, our house has but one room. Your daughter would be ashamed to live in a place as small as this."

"True," muttered the merchant. "All right, I will send carpenters to build you many rooms."

After the merchant left, Taro chuckled. "Splendid. My plan is working!"

When the widow's house was finished, the merchant asked, "Now will you consent to the marriage?"

"I fear, sir, that your daughter will still not find happiness here."

"What is it now?" cried the merchant. "Speak your mind or my daughter will turn into a clay pot!"

"My Taro has no job," said the widow. "How can he keep your daughter in luxury and comfort?"

"Surely this is the end of me," groaned the merchant. "All right, your son shall manage my storehouse. But I warn you, madam, he will have no time for naps at my place. Now do you consent to the marriage?"

Taro's mother tossed her head like a cormorant that has caught a large fish. "You have my consent," she said.

No sooner had the merchant left than the widow hurried to tell Taro the news. "The merchant has made a most wonderful offer," she cried.

Taro sat up in bed, ho-hum, stretching and yawning like a satisfied cat.

"It was all part of my plan, Mother. I hope you accepted the offer."

"Indeed I have," said his mother. "You start work first thing tomorrow morning."

"Work!" Taro leaped out of bed. "What do you mean? That was not part of my plan!"

"Ha! Do you think you are the only one who makes plans?" his mother answered.

The wedding ceremony was the finest the townfolk had ever seen. And as it turned out, the marriage is a happy one.

The ujigami must be pleased, for he has never shown himself again. And the merchant's daughter has shown no signs of turning into a pot.

As for Taro, he does a good job keeping count of the rice for his father-in-law, which is no easy task. If he is not the busiest man in town, neither is he the laziest.

It has been a long time since anyone has called Taro "The Boy of the Three-Year Nap." Perhaps everyone has forgotten by now.